# Introduction

Akbar was one of the last rulers in India who ruled well over a large portion of India. It is said that he had 9 living gems in his court. Out of these 9 gems, two are the most well-known.

Tansen, who is said to be one of the greatest singers ever to have lived, was one of these 9 living gems of Akbar's court.

And the other one was the great Birbal. It is said that Birbal was among the smartest men in the kingdom of Akbar. He was wise and knew how to reply to any kind of question or to handle any difficult question.

Soon, stories began to spread about the wisdom of Birbal.

Many of these stories are often attributed to other wise legends like the great Tenali Raman or to Gonu Jha.

How many of these stories are true and actually happened with Birbal or with Tenali or Gonu Jha? We don't know. Did any of these stories actually happen at all? We cannot be sure.

But there is one thing that we can be sure of.

These stories are interesting and entertain us. So,

let's dive into these stories. Hope you enjoy

them.

# Birbal goes
# to Heaven

One day, Emperor Akbar was having his hair cut

from the Royal Barber. Mid-way through the cut,

the Royal Barber asked the permission of the

Emperor to discuss an urgent matter with him.

"O Emperor! I saw a dream yesterday night. Your

father, the great Humayun, blessed me with his

presence in the dream. He ordered me to tell you

that he is happy in heaven and is really pleased

with how you are taking care of the kingdom."

Hearing these words from the barber, Akbar

became sad.

"What else did my great father say?" Akbar

asked.

"Your father told me that he is very happy and

content. But he says that heaven is very boring

and he wants some entertainment. If you were to

send Birbal to him, he would be very pleased.

Whenever he sees Birbal from heaven, he

becomes happy with his wit and constantly

praises Birbal's smartness."

After the haircut, Akbar asked for Birbal to come

and see him immediately.

When Birbal reached, he saw the Emperor pacing

around his room. He understood that something

is wrong.

"What concerns you, great Emperor?" Birbal

enquired.

"Birbal, I am really pleased with you. However, as

the royal barber informed me, my father in

heaven gets bored without any kind of

entertainment. Hence, he wants to meet you."
Akbar begrudgingly informed Birbal about the
discussion he had with the royal barber.

"So, my dear servant, I want you to go to heaven
and entertain my father, grandfather and other
ancestors."

Birbal gave the request some thought and
replied, "Sure, I would love to do this for the
great Emperor. However, I want you to give me a
week's time to say proper goodbyes to all my
family members. Also, another three weeks of
isolation to repent for my sins so that I reach

heaven directly. And I also wish to have my funeral in front of my house."

Akbar was pleased to see the loyalty of Birbal and rewarded him with lots of gold and jewelries. He also gave Birbal the one month he had asked for. He also instructed all ministers and courtiers to not disturb Birbal with any work in his last 3 weeks.

After the month was over, Birbal arranged for his funeral in front of his house.

He lied down on the funeral pyre and after saying proper goodbye to everyone, his son burnt the pyre.

**Birbal was dead.**

Although Akbar was really sad that his dear minister is now dead, he was happy believing that his ancestors now had someone to entertain them.

And so, months passed.

After nearly 6 months, one day when Akbar was busy with some work, Birbal suddenly came to his courtroom.

He looked same in every aspect, other than that he had a very long beard and had really long hair too. This was against his usual look where he kept no beard and medium sized hair.

Confused over this, Akbar asked him how he was back.

"Good Emperor, your father and grandfather and your other ancestors bless you. They treated me well, just like you do. And I did my best to entertain them." Birbal replied.

"That's good to know Birbal. But, how are you back? And why do you have such long hair and beard?" Akbar asked curiously.

"Dear Emperor, everything in heaven is awesome. Your ancestors are having lots of fun there. But there is a problem. There's no barber there. So, I was not able to get a haircut or get my beard shaved. And this happened within 6 months. Your ancestors have been there for ages. They are tripping over their beards and falling down while walking."

"And this is why they sent me back to earth to request you to send your royal barber to them. This way they can get the desired haircut."

Akbar immediately order the royal barber to be called. When he initially refused, Akbar ordered for him to be killed so that he can go to heaven to serve the emperor's ancestors.

Facing death, the royal barber fell on the feet of Birbal and asked for forgiveness.

Birbal asked him to ask for forgiveness from the emperor and explain to the emperor why he doesn't want to go to heaven.

The royal barber repeatedly cried in front of the Emperor and kept asking to be spared. He explained...

"My kind Emperor, our minister Birbal is the cleverest person in your court. Because of this, many ministers are very jealous of him. As you have given many rewards to Birbal, they wanted to get him killed.

For that purpose, they came to me and told me to make up the story about your father. Please forgive me."

Akbar asked the names of the ministers. After hearing their side, Akbar understood that they had tried to get Birbal killed.

The emperor ordered all of them to pay hefty fines to Birbal and they were removed from the royal court. The royal barber was sentenced with 6 months of prison.

After all this was settled, Akbar asked Birbal for forgiveness.

"But tell me Birbal. How did you survive your funeral? And why did you take the one month leave?" Akbar couldn't understand how a man could survive from fire.

"During the one month leave, I constructed a tunnel from the front of my house to a small room inside the house. During the funeral, I used the tunnel to escape. This is how I survived."

Emperor was pleased with Birbal's wisdom and gifted him with lots of treasures and jewelry.

# Counting Crows

Birbal's wisdom was unmatched in that era.

Because of this, his fame had reached far and

wide. Many kings and their ministers would want

to test his wisdom.

One day, one such learned man named Vallabh

came from the neighboring kingdom of Vidarbha.

He was the most brilliant man in the court of the

king in Vidarbha. He wanted to test if the fame

was Birbal was deserved or whether others were simply creating stories out of thin air.

To test Birbal, Vallabh came up with a question he thought could not be answered.

When Birbal came to the court on the request of Akbar, he met Vallabh.

After the normal greeting and exchange of gifts was done, Birbal asked him the purpose for his visit.

"My king wanted to see if the Emperor's minister is smart as others say. If you could answer my question, I would be able to report back to my king."

Birbal smiled at these words of Vallabh.

"What is the question, O learned one?" Birbal enquired.

"My king wants to know the exact numbers of crows in the kingdom of Emperor Akbar. Can you tell me the number of crows in your kingdom, O wise Birbal?"

Birbal was stunned at the question. No one could have expected such a question. How can one count the number of crows?

All the ministers and courtiers started murmuring among themselves. Emperor Akbar got visibly angry and was about to shout on Vallabh when he heard Birbal say something.

"Sure. I can answer the question. Just give me one day's time. Tomorrow, at this exact time, I will answer your question."

Birbal smiled, praised the emperor and left with his permission.

The next day, Birbal arrived at the designated time and stood in the middle of the court. Vallabh was waiting for him.

"So, wise Birbal, do you have the answer to my question" Vallabh was sure there was no way Birbal counted the total number of crows in the whole kingdom.

Birbal smiled and replied, "O learned Vallabh, there are a total of 353871 crows in the kingdom of the great Emperor Akbar."

Vallabh was stunned at this number.

"How can you be so sure, Birbal? What if we count the number and there are more crows in the kingdom?" Vallabh asked Birbal.

"Then, some crows may have flown in to our kingdom from the neighboring states." Birbal replied.

A stunned Vallabh found that he had no reply to this answer.

"What if the number of crows is lesser?" Vallabh asked.

"Then it means some crows from our kingdom went to other kingdoms, maybe to visit their friends and family staying in those regions"

The whole courtroom burst in laughter and Emperor Akbar couldn't stop himself from praising Birbal again and again.

An embarrassed Vallabh said, "You are telling a lie, Birbal. No one could have counted the number of crows in one day."

Birbal replied, again with a smile, "If you are unsatisfied, you can count the crows yourself. Let's see if your numbers are different. But remember, in the time it takes you to count the crows, many crows would have given birth and many would have died. How would we know?"

Vallabh understood how wise Birbal was. He accepted his defeat and went back to his kingdom.

# Fake Mother

A part of the duties of the king or the emperor was solving disputes among the citizens. Although there were local courts to help the people, sometimes the cases were too complex or the parties involved didn't agree with the decisions of the lower courts.

In all such cases, the case came up to the king or Emperor to solve. As the king was the highest authority in the land, his verdict was final.

One such curious case came into the court of Emperor Akbar.

There was a small baby, barely 4-6 months old. And there were two women fighting for the custody of the baby.

Both women claimed to be the birth mother of the child. Both of them were crying and wailing non-stop asking to be declared the mother of the child. They were both also demanding punishment for the other woman. There was huge commotion in the crowd seeing this case.

How could someone figure out who the real mother is? As both of them claimed to be the mother of the child and the child couldn't testify himself, all the ministers and even Akbar himself were unable to think of any solution to the problem.

During all this time, Birbal was silent.

Emperor Akbar asked him for his opinion.

Birbal asked the first woman to explain her side.

The first woman said, "O Wise Minister, I gave birth to this baby 5 months back. After a few days, my health deteriorated. Because of this, I asked my friend, this woman, to take care of my baby for a few days.

After few weeks, my health improved and I asked her to return my baby. She has since been claiming that this is her baby. Please help me get back my son."

Birbal gave her response some thought and then turned to the other woman. He then asked her to explain her side.

"Sir, this woman is a liar. She is mentally unstable and makes such stories to put a claim on my child. This is my child and I gave birth to it. Please let me have my child with me in peace."

Birbal heard the other side and then he came up with a plan.

Turning to the Emperor, he said, "Dear Emperor, both women claim to be the mother of this child. As we cannot find the real mother, let us give the child to both of these women."

The whole courtroom was shocked.

"Birbal, what nonsense is this? How can you give one baby to two women?" Akbar shouted angrily.

"O Emperor, have some faith in me. I will do justice to these women and the baby". Saying this, Birbal signaled Akbar to tell him that he has a plan.

Birbal then ordered one of the soldiers to take the baby from the first woman who was holding the baby.

The soldier came forward the took the baby away.

"Dear gatekeeper, please take this child to the butcher and ask him to cut it into two pieces. We will give one piece each to both of these ladies." Birbal ordered the soldier.

Hearing this, one woman fell to the feet of Birbal. "O Minister, don't do this injustice. Let the other woman have the baby. Please do not kill my baby."

She repeatedly asked Birbal and Emperor Akbar to spare her son. She was willing to let the other woman have the child.

Wailing like this for a few minutes, she fainted.

Birbal turned to the soldier and ordered the soldier to hand over the baby to the first woman.

Turning to Emperor Akbar, Birbal said, "Dear Emperor, the first woman is the real mother of the child. Only a real mother would be willing to be separated from her child if it meant that the child gets to live. Only a real mother can offer such a great sacrifice."

All the ministers hailed Birbal for his wisdom.

Akbar heavily punished the second woman and gave a hefty prize to the first woman to take care of the child.

# The Face that Brings Bad Luck

In the empire of Akbar, there lived a man named

Yusuf. When Yusuf was born, his mother died

giving birth to him. The same day, his father was

trampled by a horse.

Because of these events, people cursed him and

thought that he was unlucky.

Soon people started saying that one look at the face of Yusuf would bring great misfortune. So, wherever Yusuf went, people would not only curse him, but also throw stones at him.

As they say, fame is any kind is still fame. Soon, the story of Yusuf reached the court of Emperor Akbar.

He was curious to find out whether the tales were true. He refused to believe that a man could be so unlucky that just a look at his face would mean bad luck for you.

On the orders of the emperor, the soldiers searched for Yusuf and brought him to the court of the Emperor.

When Yusuf reached the court, Emperor Akbar began to talk to him in a nice manner. He wanted to know about the life of Yusuf.

No sooner had Yusuf begun telling his story, then a guard came into the court.

He informed the Emperor that the queen had fallen unconscious.

Hearing this, Akbar quickly went to his palace to

see the queen. He stayed with the queen

throughout the day.

In the evening, the queen's health was restored.

Akbar came back to the court.

He saw Yusuf, still standing in the court, waiting

for the emperor.

Akbar grew angry at him.

"It seems all the tales about you being unlucky is

true. One look at your face and I nearly lost the

queen. You made the queen sick." Akbar

shouted.

He then ordered the guards to take Yusuf away and throw him in a dark cell where nobody could see him.

Yusuf started shouting and protesting. He called the decision of the Emperor unfair and asked to be released. He started crying and shouting at the top of his voice, "I am innocent, O Emperor! I am innocent."

Although it was evidently clear that the decision of the Emperor was wrong, no courtier dared say this to the Emperor.

Soon, Birbal stood up, went near Yusuf, said something in his ears and returned to his chair.

Yusuf pleaded the Emperor to hear his words.

"Dear Emperor, the queen didn't see my face but fell ill. But you and many courtiers saw my face. None of them fell ill. How can I then be unlucky?"

Emperor Akbar started thinking on this.

Yusuf then added, "Further, O great king, you seeing my face made the queen ill. But because I saw your face, I am being imprisoned into some dark cell. Are you unlucky too?"

Hearing this, Akbar realized his mistake. He burst out into laughter and ordered the soldiers to release Yusuf.

Akbar also awarded Yusuf with 100 gold coins. He also asked Birbal why he couldn't advise him directly.

"I wanted you to see it from the perspective of Yusuf. There was no one to put it better then he himself." Birbal replied.

Akbar was satisfied with the reply and rewarded Birbal handsomely.

# Birbal's Khichdi

Note: - *This is one of the most famous stories of Akbar and Birbal. This is so famous that it has turned into a sort of idiom in India. 'Birbal ki Khichdi' (Birbal's Khichdi) is the idiom and you will understand the meaning by the end of this story.*

It was an unusually cold winter that year. One night, while roaming around his capital with his trusted advisor Birbal, the Emperor stood near the river. Out of curiosity, he touched the water to see the temperature.

Shivers ran down his whole body when he touched the water.

"I dare someone to stand in this water one whole night. It is impossible." Akbar said.

"Someone determined enough can do it, my lord." Birbal, who was also standing besides the Emperor, replied.

"I do not believe you Birbal. In fact, let me prove you wrong." Akbar said. He then signaled one soldier to come forward. "Get an announcement made in the whole kingdom. Whoever willingly stands in this river, near this area, for the whole night will be rewarded 1000 gold coins from my treasury."

Akbar was so confident that no one could do this task that he announced a really high reward amount for this task.

In the coming 2-3 days, hundreds of people tried to stand in the river for the whole night. But, after standing for a few minutes, all of them

withdrew from the challenge.

The next day, there were no challengers who

came forward.

On the last day of the challenge, one man named

Vishnu Pandit accepted the challenge.

The water was colder than ever and as soon as

Vishnu entered the water, he started shivering.

Somehow, he was able to stay the whole night in

the river. When the morning sun rose, the

soldiers announced Vishnu as the winner of the

contest.

Akbar asked for Vishnu to be brought to his court. Akbar treated him with respect.

"Tell me, O Vishnu. How is it that a common man like you was able to withstand the severe cold temperature of the water and stay in the whole night?" Akbar wanted to know if there was some secret.

Vishnu replied humbly, "O Great Emperor! It was difficult at first. My mind kept thinking of reasons why I should give up. But then, I saw one distant lamp burning alone in the night. Seeing it, I felt a warmth within me. I kept looking at that lamp the whole night and somehow, I survived this challenge."

Hearing this, Akbar grew angry and declared that Vishnu had cheated by using the lamp as a source of heat.

He denied Vishnu of the prize and had him jailed for cheating.

Birbal heard of this. He was sad but could not overrule the emperor.

The next evening, Birbal invited the emperor and few of the top ministers to come to his home the next evening for dinner.

They all accepted the invitation.

The next evening, all of them came to the home of Birbal. All of them started discussing state matters with each other.

After some time, everyone got hungry. They asked Birbal if the food is ready. Birbal said that it would be ready in some time.

After another hour, the emperor grew restless. He asked Birbal if the food was ready.

Birbal replied, "It will be ready soon, my emperor. I have been cooking it since this morning."

Akbar was surprised to hear this. He wanted to

see what kind of food Birbal was cooking that

required the whole day to cook.

On Akbar's request, Birbal brought him to the

place where he was cooking the food. Birbal was

cooking the food outside near a tree.

Akbar was surprised to see the scene. The pot inside which the Khichdi (an Indian dish) was cooking was hanging on one branch of a tall tree and there was fire on the ground that was supposed to cook the food.

Seeing this, Akbar angrily shouted on Birbal, "Birbal, you fool! How can the pot get any warmth from the fire that is 6 feet below it? Which idiot taught you to cook like this?"

Birbal replied, "Sir, if one man standing in water can get warmth from a lamp burning 50-100 meters away, why can this pot not get warmth from this fire just 6 feet away?"

Akbar realized his folly.

"Birbal, I get your point. But, can I have some real food now? I really am hungry."

Birbal had separately arranged for food and served the same to the emperor.

After eating the food, the Emperor personally went to have Vishnu released. He then gave Vishnu the 1000 gold coins and to top it, he also gave him another 1000 for the suffering caused because of the imprisonment.

Vishnu heavily left with the gold coins for his village.

# Akbar's lost Diamond Ring

Emperor Akbar once lost his precious diamond ring which had the largest diamond in his kingdom. He remembered seeing the diamond ring about 2-3 hours back.

But his courtroom was full of people and he couldn't figure out who had taken his ring.

It was also impossible to search each and every person effectively without making all the respected people feel disrespected.

He sought the advice of his ministers.

None of them could figure out any way to find the thief.

Birbal had gone out for some work and he came back to the court just when Akbar was about to give up.

As soon as Birbal came, Akbar summoned him to come close to his throne. He explained everything to Birbal.

Birbal scanned the room once and announced, "O Great Emperor, the thief of the diamond ring is still in the courtroom. Not only do I know he is here, I also know who it is."

The whole courtroom became silent and everyone started looking all around to see if they could identify the thief too.

Akbar shouted, "Tell me Birbal, who is the thief? I will have him beheaded."

Birbal replied, "The thief is the one with a straw stuck in his beard."

Suddenly, one of the courtiers reached for his

beard to check for a straw. As soon as Birbal saw

this, he asked the soldiers to search that man.

The diamond ring was found in one of his bags.

Emperor Akbar sent the thief to the prison and

rewarded Birbal handsomely. He praised Birbal's

wit for many days and kept repeating this story to

everyone he met.

# The Well and it's Water

Once upon a time, in the village Shyampur near

Mathura, lived a poor farmer named Hari. Hari

had been farming his land all his life and he was

somehow able to sustain himself and his family

through the land.

Near his land was a well owned by Abdul, a

cunning man who lived in Mathura. Abdul had

bought the land on which the well stood 2 years back.

Before Abdul bought the land, all the farmers used the water from the well for their crops.

But once Abdul bought the land, he didn't allow anyone to draw water from the well. The farmers had to walk miles to find another source of water to use for farming.

Hari had saved some money for his daughter's wedding. Using that money and taking some loan, Hari bought the well from Abdul at 3 times the price of the well. Abdul knew that the farmers needed the water and hence, he sold the well for such an exorbitant price.

Hari started using the water from the well for his farming.

However, one day Abdul turned up and started abusing Hari for using his water. Hari was shocked to hear this. He called for the gram Panchayat. The Gram Panchayat asked Abdul if he had sold the well to Hari. Abdul agreed.

"Then, why can't he use the water from the well?" The panch (5 judges) asked Abdul.

Abdul said, "I have sold only the well to Hari, not the water inside the well."

The panch didn't know how to counter this. Abdul started asking Hari to pay him for the water he had already used.

Hari went to the court of Emperor Akbar to ask for justice.

Finding such a weird case at hand, Emperor Akbar didn't know what to do.

So, he called Birbal and asked him to judge the case on his behalf.

Birbal asked both of them to state their case.

Hari said, "Dear Sir, I purchased this land at great cost. I paid Abdul thrice the value of the well so that the farmers can peacefully use this water. Now, Abdul says we can't use the water from the well. He comes to the village and abuses us and threatens us with harm if we use water from his well."

Saying this, Hari started crying.

"What do you have to say on this, Abdul?" Birbal asked Abdul.

"Sir, I have sold the well to Hari. I do not dispute this. He can have the well to himself. But I never entered into an agreement whereby Hari or the other farmers could use my water from the well. The water still belongs to me. If they want the water, they can buy it from me. To use the water for one month, I ask them to pay me 1 gold coin each. This is a fair price for the water, in my opinion." Abdul replied.

Birbal understood what Abdul was up to.

Birbal thought on the case for some time and gave the judgement.

"Hari, Abdul is correct. He is the legal owner of the water in the well. You have no right to the water. From here on, you will pay Abdul one gold coin every month to use the water."

Hari fell on his knees and asked Birbal for mercy. Abdul started grinning.

"Hari, I have not finished my judgement. Please wait for me to finish." Birbal smiled reassuringly at Hari.

"Dear Abdul, now that it has been established that you own the water in the well, please show me the contract where Hari has allowed you to use his premises to store your water. Whose permission have you taken to store your water in Hari's well?"

Abdul was shocked to hear this. He had no reply to this question.

"Sir... I didn't …. I didn't know such a permission was required." Abdul replied.

"So, you mean to say you don't need permission to use the premises of other people?" Birbal had cornered Abdul.

Abdul was stunned. He knew where this was going.

He fell to Birbal's feet and asked for forgiveness.

Birbal said, "As we have established that the well is the property of Hari and the water is the property of Abdul, I order Abdul to remove his water from Hari's premises by the end of today. If he fails to do so, he will pay Hari **one gold coin DAILY** as rent to use his premises."

Hari jumped with joy on hearing this judgement. He started praising Birbal's wit and thanked the emperor for such a swift and fair justice.

Abdul kept crying and asking for forgiveness but Birbal didn't budge.

Abdul asked Hari for forgiveness. He thought he could rob the poor man, but because of the brilliance of Birbal, Abdul had to pay a hefty price for his wickedness.

# Smart People Think Alike

One day, in the court of Emperor Akbar, there was a big debate going on. There were two sides in the courtroom.

One side believed that everyone follows the Emperor's orders without fail as they love the emperor.

Other side argued that some people do not follow the rules.

Birbal was silent throughout this debate.

Akbar wanted to know what the courtiers felt. So he did not intervene in the discussion. But seeing that Birbal was silent throughout the debate, Akbar asked Birbal for his opinion.

Birbal replied, "People are the same. Everyone tries to disobey the rule if it profits them and they think no one would find out."

Akbar didn't believe Birbal and asked him to prove it.

Birbal asked for a few days time from Akbar.

After some days, Birbal announced that every citizen of the capital had to come to the palace on the next no moon day. Birbal had made a large tank like a well to collect milk.

Every citizen had to pour one liter milk in the tank.

On the no moon day, everyone came as planned. There were no special lights in those times to light up the environment.

The guards were stationed far away from the tank.

People stood in line with one mug in their hands, supposedly full of milk.

One by one everyone came and poured in the 'milk'.

Next day, Birbal asked the emperor to accompany him to see how much milk they had collected.

"What do you think, dear Emperor? How many people would have cheated by pouring water instead of milk?" Birbal asked.

"There are some people who break the laws, Birbal. I am sure about 5% to 10% people would have poured in water while the remaining loyal population of my city poured milk."

Birbal didn't say anything.

Soon, they reached the tank.

When Akbar looked inside, there was nothing but clear water inside the tank.

Akbar was shocked to see this.

Birbal said, "Everyone assumed that the others in the city would act honestly. So, each of them believed that one mug of water in the tank full of milk won't change anything. People think alike. Everyone thought that the others would be honest. And hence, no one was honest. This is why the whole tank is full of water."

Now, to show the Emperor that people are honest out of the fear of retribution, Birbal again announced for the same event on the next no moon day.

This time, however, he also announced that guards would randomly check the mugs of citizens to see if they have brought milk with them or not. He also announced that the emperor would personally check the collected milk the next day.

Once more, people came at the scheduled time and started pouring in the milk.

The next day, Birbal took Akbar to see that the tank was now overflowing with pure milk.

Akbar understood that although the citizens love their emperor, they are also smart and think alike. And without the fear of being caught, all of them will try to cheat the system as much as possible.

CPSIA information can be obtained
at www.ICGtesting.com
Printed in the USA
LVHW091539031120
670591LV00007B/283

9 781794 514195